THAT'S FACTS-INATING!

AMAZING ANIMALS

Kidsbooks®

DO YOU KNOW...

CHICKENS ARE THE CLOSEST LIVING RELATIVES TO THE **T-REX?**

Tigers are good **swimmers?**

GECKOS CAN WALK UPSIDE DOWN?

Get ready to learn **tons** of other **fascinating facts** in this **fun-filled book** about **animals!**

Giraffes are the **TALLEST** land animals on **Earth.**

Boa constrictors are excellent *swimmers*.

SNOW LEOPARDS CAN'T ROAR.

Meow?

Hummingbirds
are the **only group**
of birds that
can fly **backward.**

CATS SLEEP FOR ABOUT 12 TO 16 HOURS A DAY.

It is physically **impossible** for **pigs** to **look up** at the **sky**.

A PANDA'S DIET is made up ALMOST ENTIRELY of BAMBOO.

Crocodiles do not have sweat glands, so they open their mouths to cool down.

Ants are able to carry more than **50 times** their own **weight.**

A horse's brain is about the size of a potato.

Houseflies only live for about

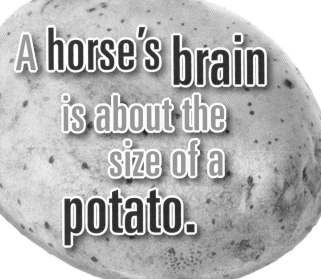

two weeks.

ONLY VENOMOUS SNAKES HAVE FANGS.

"RHINOCEROS" MEANS "NOSE HORN."

The nose knows!

Did you say something?

A giraffe can clean its ears with its tongue.

Blue-footed boobies show off their **feet** to **attract a mate**

(the **bluer** the feet, the more **attractive**).

SOME SNAILS CAN GROW ANOTHER EYE IF THEY LOSE ONE.

Honeybees communicate through *dancing.*

Snakes **smell** with their **tongues.**

Hedgehogs have about 5,000 spikes.

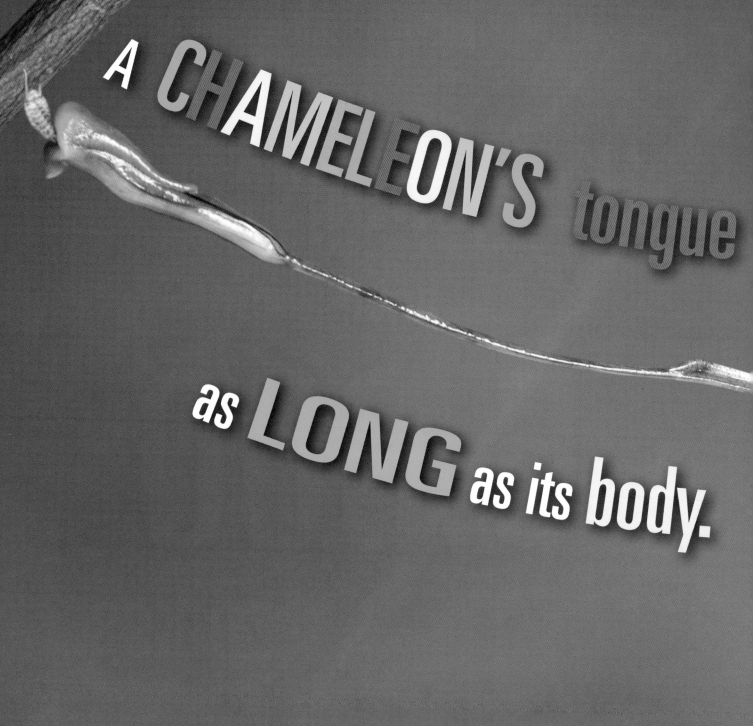

A CHAMELEON'S tongue as LONG as its body.

can be **twice**

MOST ORANGUTANS AND ADULT HUMANS HAVE THE SAME NUMBER OF TEETH (32).

Say aahhh.

Aaaaahh!

FOR THE **FIRST YEAR** OF ITS LIFE, A **BABY BLUE WHALE** GAINS ABOUT **200 POUNDS EVERY DAY.**

STARFISH HAVE EYES ON THE ENDS OF EACH OF THEIR ARMS.

Geckos lick their eyes to keep them clean.

BABY RACCOONS ARE CALLED KITS.

Female cats are called QUEENS.

Sea horses mate for life.

Giraffes have blue-black colored tongues.

"HIPPOPOTAMUS" means "RIVER HORSE" in GREEK.

Porcupines
can have
more than

30,000
quills, or
spikes.

GECKOS
CAN WALK

UPSIDE DOWN.

The largest butterfly is Queen Alexandra's birdwing, with a wingspan of up to 11 inches!

BEAVERS HAVE TRANSPARENT EYELIDS TO HELP THEM SEE UNDERWATER.

BEAVERS' TEETH NEVER STOP GROWING.

This is why they gnaw on **branches** or **sticks**—to keep their **teeth** from growing too **long**.

Jackrabbits run in a zigzag when being chased by a predator.

Cats have 32 muscles in each ear.

Ducks do not have nerves in their feet.

If they're walking on land, they can't tell if the ground feels hot or cold.

Koalas sleep for around twenty hours a day.

The **largest** parrot is the hyacinth macaw, which has a *wingspan* of

more than **four feet.**

THERE ARE OVER ONE BILLION COWS IN THE WORLD.

CHICKENS ARE THE CLOSEST LIVING RELATIVES TO THE T-REX.

Bats are the **only** *mammals* that can *fly.*

EMUS ARE BIRDS THAT CANNOT FLY.

WHAT?!? How am I supposed to get around?

Sloths move so *slowly* that sometimes ALGAE grows on their fur.

Dogs **sweat** through the pads on the bottoms of their feet.

43

The **LOGGERHEAD TURTLE** is believed to be the **LARGEST HARD-SHELLED** turtle on **EARTH.**

A **dog's nose** is like a
human fingerprint:
it is completely **unique.**

RATS CANNOT VOMIT.

The **cardinal** is the **official bird** of **SEVEN** U.S. states.

Some breeds of chickens lay colored eggs.

Besides flying, puffins use their wings to paddle through water.

NO TWO TIGERS HAVE THE SAME PATTERN OF STRIPES.

CHAMELEONS CHANGE COLORS TO DISPLAY A REACTION OR EMOTION.

Meerkats have dark patches around their eyes to help lessen the glare of the sun.

OSTRICHES HAVE **THREE** STOMACHS.

There are about **250** different types of **turtles.**

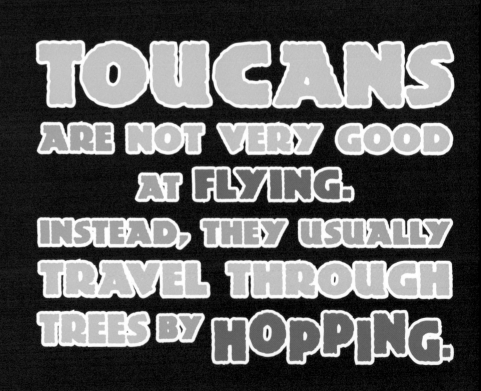

TOUCANS ARE NOT VERY GOOD AT FLYING. INSTEAD, THEY USUALLY TRAVEL THROUGH TREES BY HOPPING.

A
LION'S
ROAR

CAN BE HEARD
FROM

FIVE MILES
AWAY.

MOST SPIDERS HAVE EIGHT EYES.

BATS SLEEP HANGING UPSIDE DOWN.

A LEOPARD'S spots are called ROSETTES.

A **blue whale's** **heart** is about the size of a **small car.**

OSTRICHES HAVE THE **LARGEST EYES** OF ANY LAND ANIMAL.

Ants do not have lungs.

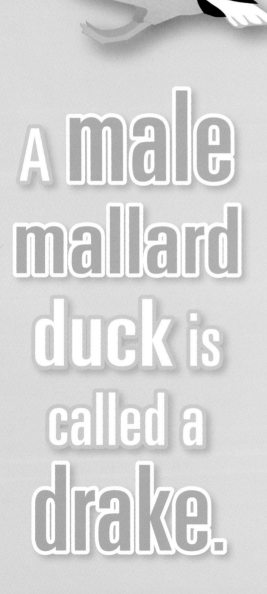

A male mallard duck is called a drake.

A FEAR of SNAKES is called OPHIDIOPHOBIA.

SEA OTTERS HAVE A **POCKET** OF **SKIN** ON THEIR **ARMS** WHERE THEY **STORE ROCKS** TO USE TO **CRACK OPEN** SHELLS OF THEIR **PREY.**

Only
male cardinals
are **bright red.**

Females are
tan or **gray.**

ELEPHANTS CAN SMELL WATER FROM MILES AWAY.

Jellyfish will evaporate in the sun because they are 98% water.

One GOLDEN POISON DART FROG has enough VENOM to KILL ♟♟♟♟♟ TEN ♟♟♟♟♟ ADULT HUMANS.

A cat's heart beats about twice the rate of a human heart.

GIRAFFE HAIR is about TEN TIMES THICKER than HUMAN HAIR.

Bulls are COLOR BLIND.

When **bullfighters** traditionally wave a **red flag**, it is the **motion** that makes the bull **angry**, not the color.

Spiders are not classified as insects. They are **arachnids,** like **scorpions** and **ticks.**

The **red flap** of skin **under** a **rooster's** beak is called a **wattle.**

A **skunk** can **spray** a target **twelve feet** away.

DOLPHINS

call each other by "names"
(specific sounds for different dolphins).

Camels can carry 400 POUNDS on their backs.

TIGERS, unlike other cats, like to swim (and they swim well).

THERE ARE ABOUT 17,500 DIFFERENT SPECIES OF BUTTERFLIES IN THE WORLD.

Ostriches can sprint over **40** miles per hour.

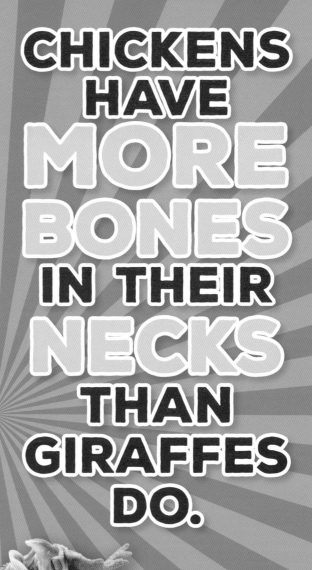

CHICKENS HAVE MORE BONES IN THEIR NECKS THAN GIRAFFES DO.

That's one long neck!

Chimpanzees use sticks and stones as tools (similar to how humans use tools).

A GROUP OF PUGS IS CALLED A GRUMBLE.

DIFFERENT TYPES OF COWS MAKE DIFFERENT KINDS OF MILK.

Female **bumblebees** have built-in "baskets" on their legs in which to carry pollen.

KOMODO DRAGONS

ARE THE

LARGEST LIZARDS
IN THE WORLD.

BATS MAKE UP ONE-FIFTH OF THE WORLD'S MAMMALS.

Snakes do not **blink** because they do not have **eyelids.**

A NARWHAL'S HORN CAN GROW TO BE ABOUT TEN FEET LONG.

The AGE of a **MOUNTAIN GOAT** can be determined by **COUNTING** the **NUMBER** of **RINGS** on its **HORNS.**

CAMELS HAVE 3 EYELIDS ON EACH EYE— THE THIRD EYELID PROTECTS THEIR EYES FROM THE DESERT SAND.

The **fennec fox** is the **world's** smallest fox, **weighing just** a little over **two pounds.**

AN OCTOPUS'S BLOOD IS BLUE.

GOATS HAVE RECTANGULAR PUPILS.

A blue whale's **tongue** can **weigh** as much as an **elephant.**

PENGUINS CANNOT BREATHE UNDERWATER.

GREYHOUNDS
are the FASTEST

DOGS

in the WORLD.

Chimpanzees are almost ·············· genetically ·············· identical to humans.

Crocodiles cannot stick their tongues out.

ELEPHANTS CAN'T JUMP.

HAMSTERS CANNOT SWIM.

BUTTERFLIES TASTE WITH THEIR FEET.

TURTLES DON'T have OUTER EARS.

HUH?

A group of goats is called a trip.

SCALLOPS have EYES.
Depending on the species, they could have between
30 and
100.

Zebras' STRIPES protect them from PREDATORS.

When zebras are in a HERD, the stripes blend together and make it hard for a predator to pick out only ONE.

DOGS can HEAR

TWICE as **FAR AWAY** as humans can.

CAT PEE GLOWS UNDER A BLACK LIGHT.

GREAT HORNED OWLS prey on ANIMALS much LARGER than themselves, such as DOGS, SKUNKS, and FALCONS.

POLAR BEARS CAN SMELL FOOD FROM ABOUT A MILE AWAY.

A chipmunk can gather up to **165 acorns** in a single day.

A group of **cats** is called a **clowder.**

The **blobfish** was once voted the

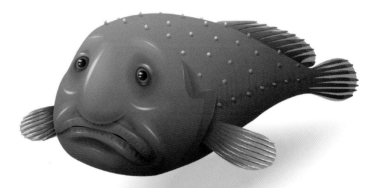

world's ugliest animal.

The hair of a **POLAR BEAR** is not actually

WHITE—it's **CLEAR**!

It looks white when the **SUN SHINES** on the hair.

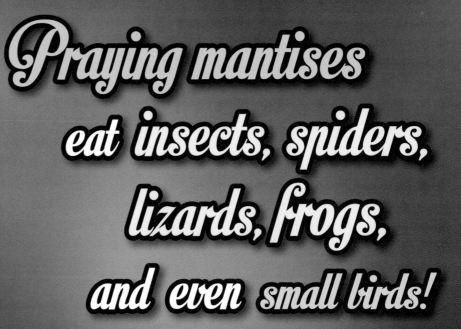

Praying mantises eat insects, spiders, lizards, frogs, and even small birds!

FLAMINGOS
EAT WITH
THEIR HEADS

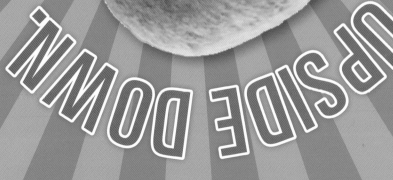

UPSIDE DOWN!

OCTOPUSES HAVE THREE HEARTS.

PANDAS SPEND ABOUT 12 HOURS A DAY EATING.

KOALAS ARE ABLE TO EAT EUCALYPTUS LEAVES, WHICH ARE POISONOUS TO OTHER ANIMALS. THIS IS BECAUSE THEY HAVE BACTERIA IN THEIR STOMACHS THAT BREAKS DOWN TOXINS.

The **fear** of **chickens** is called **alektrorophobia.**

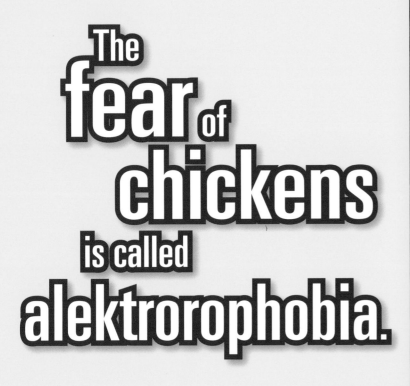

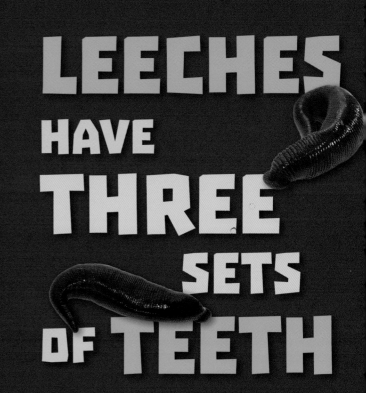

LEECHES HAVE THREE SETS OF TEETH (300 TOTAL).

Some turtles breathe through their butts.

THE **PEREGRINE FALCON** IS THE *FASTEST* ANIMAL, FLYING OVER **200** MILES PER HOUR.

BATS live TOGETHER in COLONIES of between 100 and 1,000 other bats.

The **howler monkey** is the **loudest** land animal—their **calls** can be **heard** up to **three miles away!**

ALL **SPIDERS** HAVE **FANGS.**

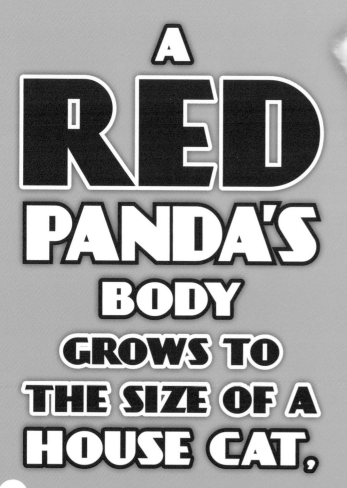

A **RED** PANDA'S BODY GROWS TO THE SIZE OF A HOUSE CAT,

SNOWY OWLS SWALLOW THEIR PREY WHOLE.

NOT INCLUDING THE RED PANDA'S BIG BUSHY TAIL THAT ADDS AN EXTRA 18 INCHES TO ITS LENGTH.

The **HEAVIEST SNAKE** in the **WORLD** is the **GREEN ANACONDA.**

It can WEIGH about 550 POUNDS.

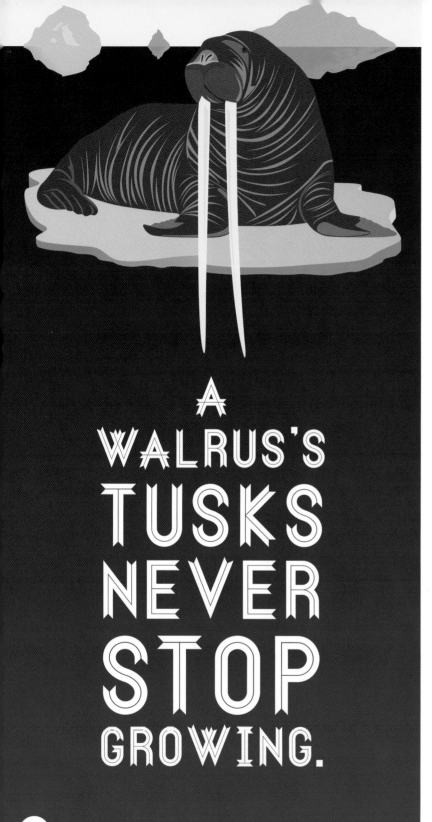

A WALRUS'S TUSKS NEVER STOP GROWING.

Humans and slugs share 70% of the same DNA.

GOATS EAT POISON IVY.

Spider silk is one of the strongest materials in the world.

A GROUP OF FROGS

IS CALLED AN ARMY.

SCIENTISTS WHO STUDY ANIMALS ARE CALLED ZOOLOGISTS.

An **anteater's** tongue can **stretch out** to more than **two feet long—** the length of **two rulers put together!**

SNAKE SCALES ARE MADE UP OF LAYERS OF CELLS STACKED ON TOP OF EACH OTHER.

THERE ARE AN ESTIMATED

400 MILLION DOGS

IN THE WORLD.

HUMMINGBIRDS ARE THE SMALLEST BIRDS IN THE WORLD.

HIPPOPOTAMUSES secrete an oily red substance that acts as SUN BLOCK.

An ostrich's eye is bigger than its brain.

TARANTULAS CAN SURVIVE FOR UP TO TWO YEARS WITHOUT FOOD.

This better last awhile.

Unlike domestic cats, tigers can only *purr* when they *exhale*.

A TURTLE'S SHELL IS MADE UP OF OVER 50 CONNECTING BONES.

Hedgehogs can eat some poisonous plants that do not hurt them. They then lick their spikes to spread the poison, which will protect them from predators.

COWS ARE FEMALE.

BULLS, STEERS, AND STAGS ARE MALE.

I'm a wise old owl!

MALE SNOWY OWLS BECOME WHITER AS THEY GROW OLDER.

WHEN MOOSE ARE FRIGHTENED, THEIR HAIR STANDS STRAIGHT UP.

Kangaroos cannot walk backward.

BURROWING OWLS GET THEIR **NAME** BECAUSE THEY **LIVE** UNDERGROUND.

AN AVERAGE CHICKEN LAYS ABOUT 260 EGGS A YEAR.

GOLDFISH
CAN LOSE THEIR COLOR
WHEN
NOT EXPOSED TO
ENOUGH
LIGHT.

UNLIKE MANY OTHER BEARS, POLAR BEARS DO NOT HIBERNATE.

THE KING COBRA HAS VENOM

POWERFUL ENOUGH TO KILL AN ELEPHANT.

WOLVERINES ARE THE LARGEST MEMBERS OF THE WEASEL FAMILY.

Sea horses are the *only species* in which the *male* bears the *unborn young.*

In ancient Britain, dogs such as mastiffs fought side by side with their owners during battle.

FULL-GROWN **BLACK RHINOS** HAVE NO **NATURAL PREDATORS** BECAUSE THEY ARE SO **BIG.**

HUMANS and **ARMADILLOS** are the **ONLY TWO** animals in the world known to have **contracted LEPROSY.**

The position of a horse's ears indicates its mood.

153

A LEOPARD'S TAIL IS ABOUT

AS LONG AS ITS BODY.

Blue-tongued skinks get their name from the **blue tongue** they **stick out** to **scare** away **predators.**

HORNED LIZARDS SHOOT **BLOOD** FROM THEIR **EYES** TO **PROTECT** THEMSELVES.

BEES CAN BE FOUND ON EVERY CONTINENT ON EARTH EXCEPT ANTARCTICA.

A GROUP OF PORCUPINES IS CALLED A **PRICKLE.**

WHEN THEY ARE BORN, PANDAS ARE SMALLER THAN MICE.

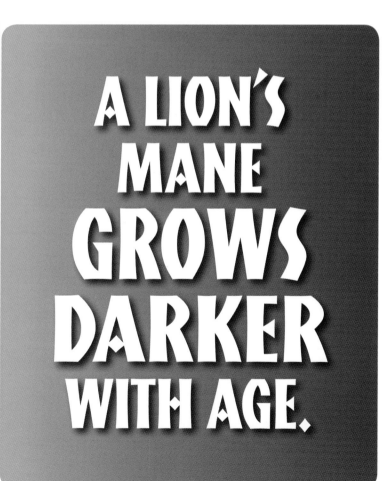

A LION'S MANE GROWS DARKER WITH AGE.

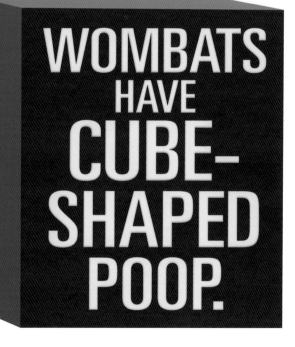

WOMBATS HAVE CUBE-SHAPED POOP.

Houseflies always hum in the key of F.

Joeys, or kangaroo babies, are about the size of lima beans when they are born.

LIONESSES ARE BETTER **HUNTERS** THAN MALE LIONS.

PENGUINS HAVE A SPECIAL GLAND THAT REMOVES SALT FROM WATER, SO THEY ARE ABLE TO DRINK DIRECTLY FROM THE OCEAN.

COWS MAY HAVE DIFFERENT ACCENTS DEPENDING ON WHERE THEY LIVE.

MOO!

MUU!

MEU!

New trees **GROW** every year because **squirrels** **forget** where they buried their **acorns.**

The name of a baby peacock

is a peachick.

HARP SEALS CAN STAY UNDERWATER FOR UP TO FIFTEEN MINUTES WITHOUT COMING UP FOR A BREATH.

JAGUARS get their name from the NATIVE AMERICAN word YAGUAR, MEANING "he who KILLS with ONE LEAP."

KANGAROO MOMS keep their BABIES, called JOEYS, in a POUCH on their BELLY for about TEN MONTHS.

PUPPIES ARE BORN BLIND, DEAF, AND TOOTHLESS.

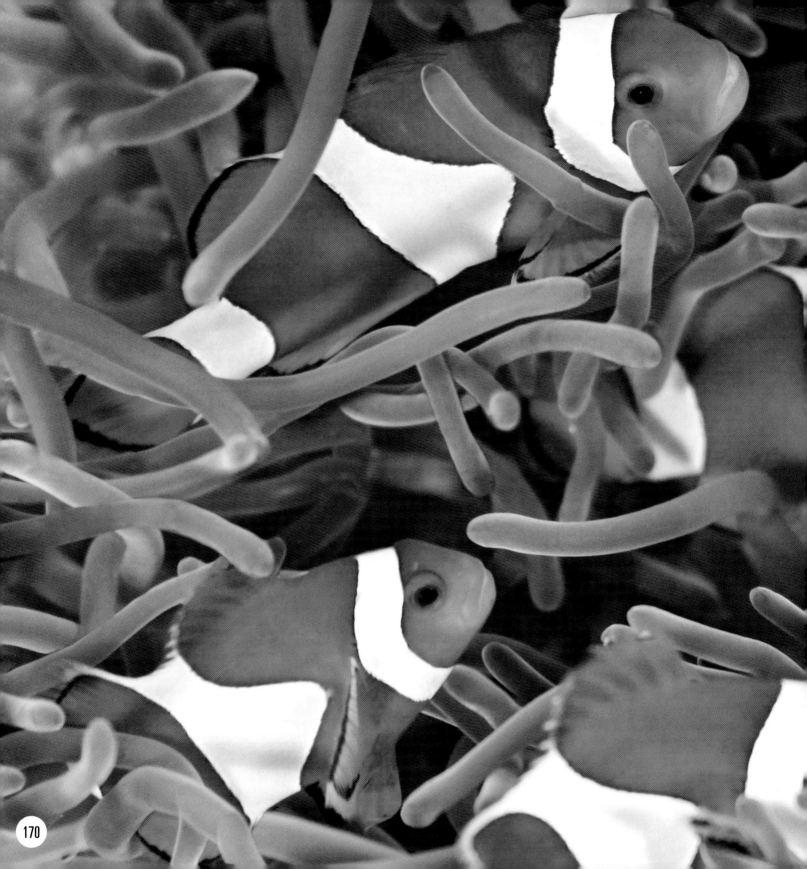

ALL CLOWNFISH ARE BORN MALE.

THEY DEVELOP INTO FEMALES AND CAN ALTERNATE BETWEEN SEXES.

There are about 700 species of venomous snakes in the world.

SPIDERS HAVE FORTY-EIGHT KNEES.

GIRAFFES ARE RUMINANTS, WHICH MEANS THEY HAVE MORE THAN ONE STOMACH.

THEY ACTUALLY HAVE **FOUR.**

THE **WATER DEER** IS OFTEN CALLED THE **VAMPIRE DEER** BECAUSE OF ITS **TWO LONG, DOWNWARD-POINTING TUSKS.**

THE AZTECS USED TO BURY CHIHUAHUAS WITH THE DEAD, AS THEY BELIEVED THE DOGS HAD THE POWER TO GUIDE HUMAN SOULS THROUGH THE UNDERWORLD.

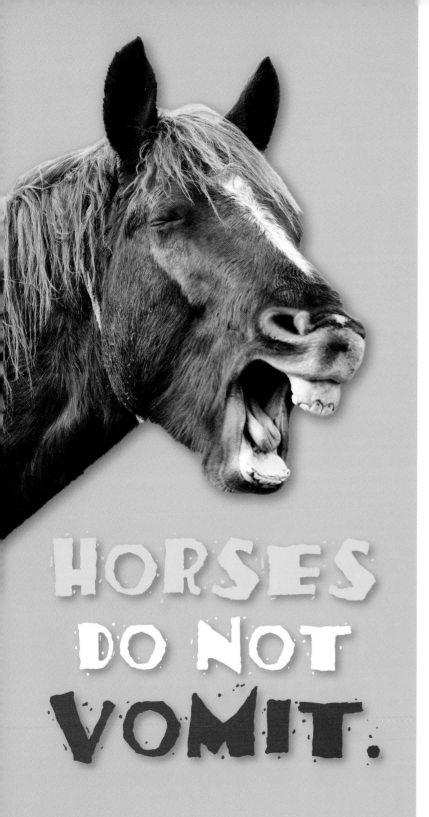

HORSES DO NOT VOMIT.

DESPITE THEIR NAME, **BLACK BEARS** COME IN **MANY COLORS** OTHER THAN **BLACK:**

BROWN, BLONDE, CINNAMON, BLUE-GREY, AND EVEN WHITE.

Sheep's wool is the most commonly used **fiber** in the world.

RACCOONS USE THEIR FINGERS TO OPEN DOORS, EAT FOOD, AND PICK UP OBJECTS, SIMILAR TO THE WAY HUMANS USE THEIR HANDS.

STARFISH, ALSO CALLED SEA STARS, are not actually fish. They are closely related to sand dollars.

THE NAME "AARDVARK" COMES FROM THE SOUTH AFRICAN LANGUAGE OF AFRIKAANS AND MEANS "EARTH PIG."

Who are you calling a pig?

ZEBRA STRIPES ARE LIKE HUMAN FINGERPRINTS— NO TWO ARE EXACTLY ALIKE.

A GROUP OF **CHICKENS** IS CALLED A **CLUTCH,** A **BROOD,** OR A **FLOCK.**

The **golden** **poison dart frog** is about the **size** of a small paper clip.

Snakes have between **200-300** vertebrae (**Humans** only have **33!**).

THE RATIO OF ANTS TO HUMANS IS ONE MILLION TO ONE.

FLEAS CAN JUMP UP TO 200 TIMES

THEIR OWN HEIGHT.

Seagulls stomp their feet on the ground to make it sound like rainfall so that earthworms will come to the surface.

DOLPHINS HAVE EYES ON THE SIDES OF THEIR HEADS WHICH GIVES THEM ALMOST 360 DEGREES OF VISION.

GREEN IGUANAS CAN **DETACH** THEIR **TAILS** AND **GROW** NEW ONES.

Squirrels will adopt the abandoned babies of their relatives.

A WALRUS'S SKIN CHANGES COLORS BASED ON THE OUTSIDE TEMPERATURE.

Male platypuses have **spurs** on their **paws** that release **toxic venom.**

AMPHIBIANS MOLT, OR SHED THEIR SKIN, AND SOME EVEN EAT THE SKIN AFTERWARD TO GAIN NUTRIENTS.

A GROUP of TIGERS IS CALLED AN AMBUSH OR STREAK.

FROGS DO NOT DRINK WATER— THEY ABSORB IT THROUGH THEIR SKIN.

OSTRICHES DO NOT HAVE TEETH. THEY SWALLOW PEBBLES TO HELP GRIND THEIR FOOD.

THE WORD "AMPHIBIAN" MEANS "TWO LIVES" AND REFERS TO THE FACT THAT THEY LIVE ON BOTH LAND AND WATER.

KANGAROOS CAN HOP 30 FEET AND TRAVEL MORE THAN 30 MILES PER HOUR.

SPIDER SIZES
CAN RANGE FROM
10 INCHES
ACROSS TO SMALLER THAN THE
HEAD OF A PIN.

I'm just soooooo tired...

DOLPHINS MUST CONSCIOUSLY SWIM TO THE WATER'S SURFACE IN ORDER TO BREATHE.

BECAUSE OF THIS, THEY ARE NEVER ABLE TO FULLY SLEEP.

Once they have **bitten** their prey, **vampire bats** spend about **30minutes** **drinking** the **blood.**

CHICKENS ARE THE WORLD'S MOST COMMON SPECIES OF BIRD.

BLACK-FOOTED FERRETS

SPEND ABOUT **90%** OF THEIR TIME UNDERGROUND.

Baby rabbits are **born** blind.

A fear of *spiders* is called ARACHNOPHOBIA.

WHEN THEY SLEEP, OTTERS HOLD HANDS TO KEEP FROM DRIFTING APART.

When giraffes fight, they swing their **long necks** at their opponents to land blows that can be heard from over **325 feet** away!

TURTLES HAVE EXISTED FOR MORE THAN 200 MILLION YEARS.

WHALE SHARKS ARE THE WORLD'S LARGEST FISH.

A group of **rattlesnakes** is called a **rhumba** or **rumba**.

LET'S DANCE!

LIONS LIVE TO BE AROUND TWELVE YEARS OLD.

HARP SEALS CAN DIVE 600 FEET INTO THE OCEAN.

Many black bears **HIBERNATE,** which means they are **INACTIVE** during the cold days of winter.

During their **HIBERNATION,** they go **without eating for** up to **SEVEN MONTHS!**

Cottontail rabbits molt (shed) twice a year.

CHINCHILLAS CAN JUMP UP TO SIX FEET IN THE AIR.

HORSES AND HUMANS HAVE ALMOST THE SAME NUMBER OF BONES.

HORSES HAVE 205.

HUMANS HAVE 206.

MALE RINGTAIL LEMURS HAVE **SCENT GLANDS** ON THEIR WRISTS AND **FOREARMS.** THEY USE THEM FOR **"STINK FIGHTS"** WITH OTHER MALES IN WHICH THEY **WIPE THEIR TAILS** ACROSS THOSE **GLANDS** AND THEN WAVE THEIR TAILS AT EACH OTHER.

KANGAROOS
LIVE IN GROUPS
CALLED MOBS.

A TURTLE'S SHELL IS ATTACHED TO ITS **SPINE**, WHICH MEANS IT CAN FEEL **PAIN** THROUGH ITS **SHELL**.

BOTH MALE AND FEMALE CARIBOU GROW ANTLERS.

ONLY MALES GROW ANTLERS IN MOST OTHER SPECIES OF DEER.

HYENAS ARE MORE CLOSELY RELATED TO CATS THAN DOGS.

Koalas are NOT CLASSIFIED as BEARS. They are MARSUPIALS, which are mammals with a POUCH used to carry newborn babies.

CATS ARE UNABLE TO TASTE ANYTHING SWEET.

POLAR BEARS HAVE BLACK SKIN TO HELP THEM ABSORB THE HEAT FROM THE SUN.

Arctic foxes have fur that **changes colors** to help them **blend** with their surroundings **in different seasons—** **white** in **winter**, **tan** or **brown** in **summer**.

ECHIDNAS ROLL UP INTO A BALL, WITH ONLY THEIR SPIKY SPINES VISIBLE, IN ORDER TO PROTECT THEMSELVES.

A HORSE'S EYES ARE 9 TIMES LARGER THAN A HUMAN'S.

HORSES HAVE THE LARGEST EYES OF ANY LAND MAMMAL.

RAVENS USE COOPERATIVE HUNTING TECHNIQUES. IF THE PREY IS TOO LARGE FOR JUST ONE OF THEM TO HUNT, THEY WILL WORK TOGETHER.

GIANT ANTEATERS HAVE NO TEETH.

The main difference between **apes** and **monkeys** is that apes **do not have tails,** but most monkeys do.

INVERTEBRATES ARE ANIMALS

THAT DO NOT HAVE BACKBONES.

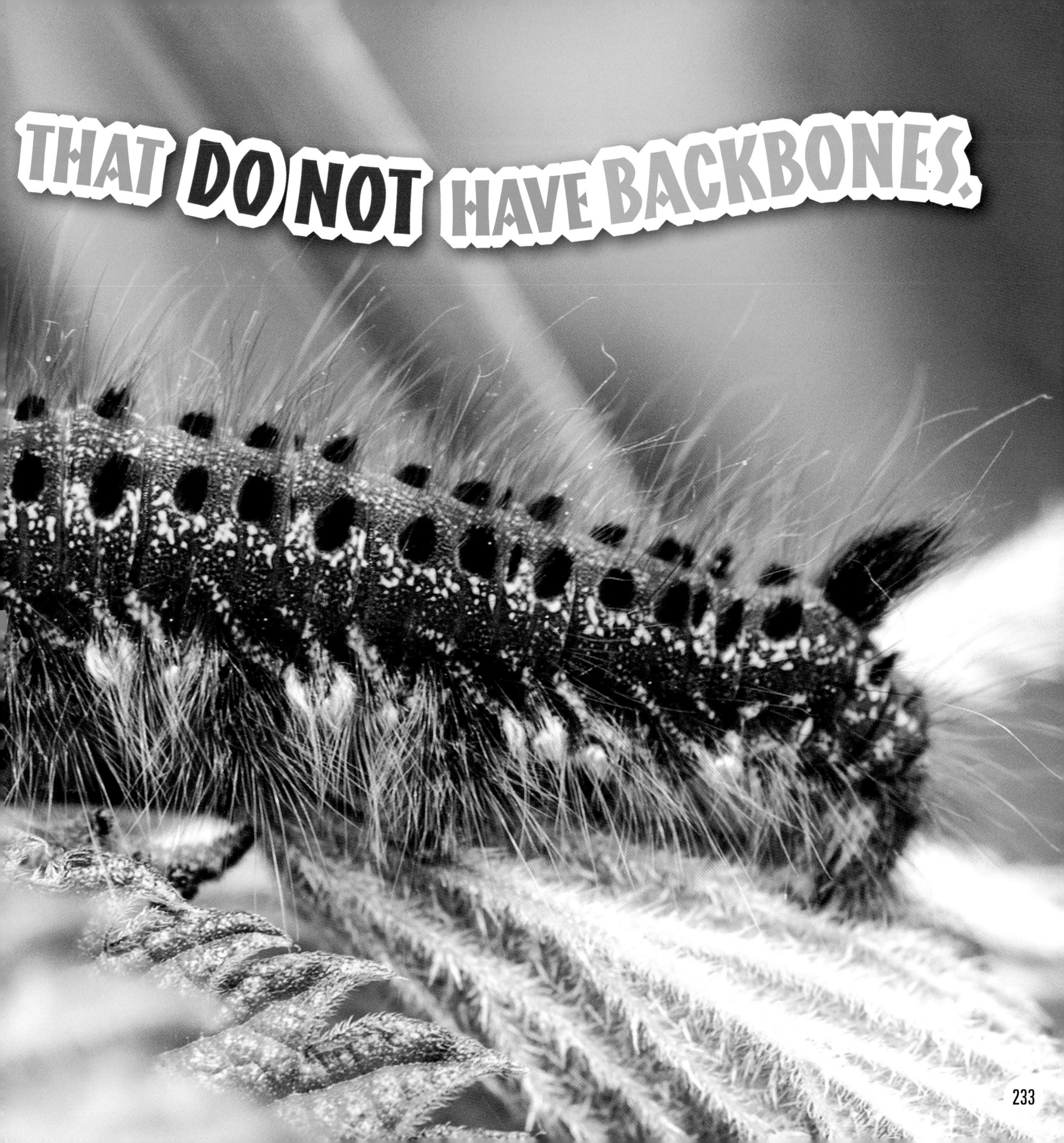

The long "tusk" of a narwhal is actually a long tooth.

That's one long tooth!

BASILISK LIZARDS
ARE ABLE TO *RUN ACROSS* WATER.

In the United States, there are about 74 MILLION PET DOGS

AND 88 MILLION PET CATS.

STARFISH DON'T HAVE BRAINS.

If a certain type of worm,
called the **planarian**,
is **split** into pieces—

halves, quarters, etc.—
each piece will turn into
a **whole new worm.**

DOGS HAVE AROUND 1,700 TASTE BUDS WHILE CATS ONLY HAVE AROUND 475.

The nine-banded armadillo almost **always** gives **birth** to **identical quadruplets.**

THERE IS A TYPE OF JELLYFISH THAT IS ABLE TO CONSTANTLY REGENERATE ITSELF SO MUCH THAT IT IS PRACTICALLY IMMORTAL.

IN SOUTHERN JAPAN, THERE IS AN ISLAND POPULATED BY HUNDREDS OF FRIENDLY RABBITS THAT WILL SWARM PEOPLE FOR FOOD.

RABBITS ARE CREPUSCULAR, WHICH MEANS THEY ARE MOST **ACTIVE** AT **DAWN** AND **DUSK.**

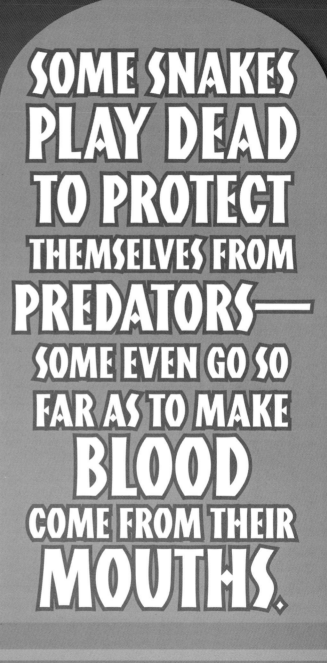

SOME SNAKES PLAY DEAD TO PROTECT THEMSELVES FROM **PREDATORS—** SOME EVEN GO SO FAR AS TO MAKE **BLOOD** COME FROM THEIR **MOUTHS.**

A PUFFIN'S FEATHERS HAVE SPECIAL OILS THAT MAKE THEM

WATERPROOF.

BALD EAGLE BABIES ARE CALLED EAGLETS.

WOLVERINES HAVE SUCH STRONG TEETH THAT THEY OFTEN EAT THE BONES AND TEETH OF THEIR PREY.

GIRAFFES DON'T HAVE VOCAL CORDS.

PIT VIPERS ARE NAMED FOR THE **PIT ORGAN** BETWEEN THEIR **EYES** AND **NOSTRILS** THAT **SENSES HEAT** FROM OTHER **ANIMALS** SO THEY KNOW WHERE TO **ATTACK.**

African elephants
communicate with

a frequency that **cannot be heard** by humans.

Reindeer change the color of their eyes based on the season.

A BABY GOAT IS CALLED A KID.

LEATHERBACK SEA TURTLES CAN WEIGH OVER 2,000 POUNDS!

SHARKS EXISTED BEFORE DINOSAURS.